To Kyle and Tyrell, my family

www.beastquest.co.uk

ORCHARD BOOKS
338 Euston Road, London NW1 3BH
Orchard Books Australia
Level 17/207 Kent St, Sydney, NSW 2000

A Paperback Original
First published in Great Britain in 2007

Beast Quest is a registered trademark of Beast Quest Limited
Series created by Beast Quest Limited, London

Text © Beast Quest Limited 2007
Cover illustration © David Wyatt 2007
Inside illustrations © Orchard Books 2007

ISBN 978 1 84616 484 2

33 35 37 39 40 38 36 34

Printed in Great Britain by the CPI Group (UK) Ltd, Croydon, CR0 4YY

The paper and board used in this paperback are natural recyclable
products made from wood grown in sustainable forests. The
manufacturing processes conform to the environmental regulations of
the country of origin.

Orchard Books is a division of Hachette Children's Books,
an Hachette Livre UK company.

www.hachette.co.uk

ARCTA
THE MOUNTAIN GIANT

BY ADAM BLADE

ORCHARD

THE ICY

THE NORTHERN
MOUNTAINS

T

WESTERN OCEAN

THE FOREST
OF FEAR

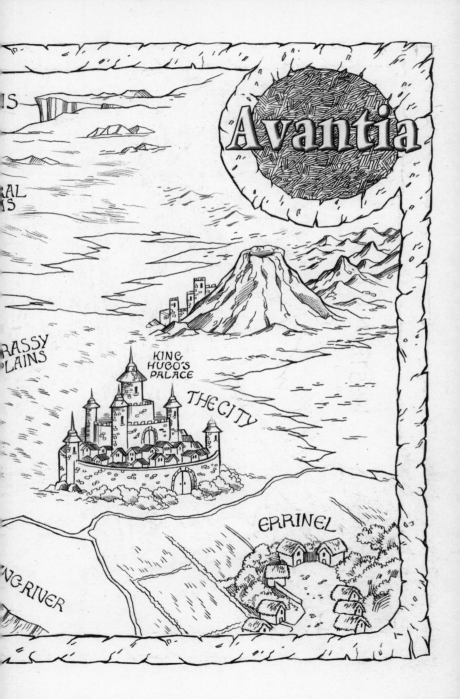

Welcome to the kingdom of Avantia. I am *Aduro* – a good wizard residing in the palace of King *Hugo*. You join us at a difficult time. Let me explain...

It is written in the Ancient Scripts that our peaceful kingdom shall one day be plunged into peril.

Now that time has come.

Under the evil spell of Malvel the Dark Wizard, six Beasts – fire dragon, sea serpent, mountain giant, horse-man, snow monster and flame bird – run wild and destroy the land they once protected.

Avantia is in great danger.

The Ancient Scripts also predict an unlikely hero. It is written that a boy shall take up the Quest to free the Beasts from the curse and save the kingdom.

We do not know who this boy is, only that his time has come...

We pray our young hero will have the courage and the heart to take up the Quest. Will you join us as we wait and watch?

Avantia salutes you,

Aduro

PROLOGUE

The caravan of wagons moved slowly along the high mountain road. As the road became steeper, the horses struggled to pull the wagons, which were loaded with food and supplies for the trading town in the mountains.

"How much longer?" a boy in the first wagon asked impatiently.

His father looked ahead at the narrow, winding road as it snaked up the mountain. It was a dangerous route, surrounded by trees, and rocks were scattered everywhere, as if there had been many landslides. "Be patient, Jack," he said. "Once we get to the pass, it's not much further." He pointed to a ridge in the distance.

Jack looked. Above the ridge, dark clouds were gathering, casting long shadows down the mountainside. The air began to cool as the sun disappeared behind the clouds.

As the wagons rounded a bend in the road, a fierce mountain wind hit them. The boy shivered and pulled his coat tighter.

"We'd better hurry if we're going to beat this storm," Jack's father called to the other traders, his voice almost lost in the wind. "We don't want to get trapped here and freeze to death."

They pushed on. But the wind seemed to gain in strength and was soon screaming through the trees.

Suddenly a thunderous crash echoed through the valley. The ground began to shake. All the wagons stopped, and the traders looked around in confusion.

"What was that?" one said.

Then they heard a deep rumbling sound and the loud crack of splintering wood, as if a tree were being snapped in half.

"What's happening?" Jack asked, trying to halt the panic in his voice.

His father looked towards the ridge. "I don't know, son," he said.

It was the first time Jack had seen fear in his father's eyes, and it sent shivers down his spine.

The ground now trembled so violently that it was hard not to fall off the wagons. The horses began to rear up, trying to escape from their harnesses. One wagon broke away and started to slide back down the mountain road, its contents spilling everywhere. Men dived out of the way as heavy barrels tumbled towards them. Then, in front of the wagons, huge boulders tore through the trees and crashed across the narrow road, just missing Jack and his father.

The road ahead was blocked!

The crashing grew louder.

Then, above them on the ridge, something appeared. In the chaos Jack was the only one to see it.

It was a giant Beast, as tall as the trees.

"Run!" Jack yelled. "Run for your lives!"

CHAPTER ONE

A NEW ADVENTURE

Tom and Elenna stopped at a fork
in the road. The road to the east led
towards the farmland of Avantia.
The road to the north would guide
them into the kingdom's mighty
mountains.

Tom knew which one they needed
to take to find the next Beast in
their Quest. He feared this mission

was going to be even more dangerous than the last. Behind him, he felt Elenna shiver as she looked at the mountain peaks in the distance, wrapped in dark, ominous clouds.

"Let's go, Elenna. We'll be all right," Tom said. Then, sensing his friend's nervousness, he added with a smile, "I mean, I've got you and the mutt for protection, haven't I?"

"The mutt? Well, thank you *very* much!" Elenna whistled to her pet wolf, Silver, who was sniffing some bushes nearby. "Come on, boy – let's teach our friend some manners!"

She pointed at Tom, and the wolf bounded across and playfully nipped his heels.

"Ow!" Tom cried.

"Take it back!" Elenna demanded.

"All right! All right! I take it back!" Tom laughed.

Elenna gave another short whistle. Silver immediately left Tom alone and trotted obediently by Storm's side.

Tom smiled. They were in this together.

The four of them set out on the road to the north.

Before he'd met Elenna, Tom had been chosen by King Hugo and his royal adviser, Wizard Aduro, for this Quest. He was to save the kingdom of Avantia from Beasts who had been trapped by the evil spell of Malvel the Dark Wizard and were destroying the land. Tom's mission was to free them from the curse, so that they could protect Avantia once more.

He wished with all his heart that his father, Taladon the Swift, could see him as he took part in the biggest adventure of his life. But his father had disappeared when he was a baby.

Before the Quest, Tom thought the Beasts only existed in legend. But now that he had fought and freed two of them himself – Ferno the Fire Dragon and Sepron the Sea Serpent – he knew just how real they were, and how deadly they could be.

So far he and Elenna had survived by working together. Now they had to face a new danger that lurked in the mountains of the north.

Arcta the Mountain Giant.

They travelled north through the foothills for some time, then Tom brought Storm to a halt. The trail before them led up a steep hill, surrounded by boulders and trees. "Let's check we're going the right way," he said. He fumbled for the magic map Wizard Aduro had given him and unrolled it. Pine trees and mountains rose up from the old parchment, standing as tall as Tom's thumbnail. The path they were following glowed.

"Another day's ride and we should reach the town," Elenna said, peering over his shoulder.

Tom looked closely at the map. The town was surrounded by five jagged mountains, and the road leading to it was long and winding. One part looked blocked by a landslide. He touched it and a plume of dust rose up from the map. They might have to find another way round. Tom had never tried to climb a mountain before. Would it be as steep and as dangerous as he imagined?

"We'd better make camp soon," he

said. "We're going to need all our energy to get up that mountain pass tomorrow."

They continued up the hill. At the top they stopped suddenly. Mountains stretched as far as they could see. Dark shadows filled the folds and gullies, while the summits seemed to blaze in the late afternoon sun. Like rows of sharp teeth, the mountains stood out against the deep-blue sky.

"It's beautiful," whispered Elenna.

Tom nodded. He'd seen many things on his Quest so far, but no landscape as breathtaking as this.

They noticed a ragged group of men coming down the trail towards them. Tom gripped his sword.

One of the men called out a greeting as they drew near. Tom could see he was carrying a young boy over his shoulder.

When the group reached them, Tom and Elenna saw that the men were traders. But they looked dirty and tired, and the boy appeared to be injured – his head was wrapped in a bloody strip of cloth.

"Can you help us?" the man carrying the boy asked. "Do you have any water? All our supplies have been destroyed."

Tom immediately passed him his water canteen. "What happened?"

"We were part of a trading caravan, bringing supplies to the town," the man explained, setting the boy down and giving him some water. "There was a landslide and we were lucky to survive."

"What triggered it?" asked Elenna.

"We don't know. The mountains are usually very stable. But the weather was odd and—"

"The giant..." spluttered the injured boy. "It was a giant..."

Tom and Elenna exchanged glances.

"Don't mind Jack," one of the men said quietly. "He got a bump on the head."

The first man said grimly, "I hope you two aren't going into the mountains."

"I'm afraid we are," said Tom.

"The mountains are dangerous, even in the best conditions," he warned, looking concerned. "The main road is blocked now and the weather's bad. I'd turn back. That's what we're doing."

"We don't have a choice," Tom said bravely.

"Well, if you must go, take this." The trader handed Tom a short length of rope. "It's not much, but it's all I have in return for your kindness. It may come in handy."

"Thank you," said Tom.

They gave the traders some more of their water and all the food they could spare, then said goodbye.

"Beware of the giant..." the young boy called back, as the traders made their way south.

Tom, Elenna, Storm and Silver pressed north. Soon the sky grew dark. It began to drizzle and the ground became muddy.

"We'd better hurry up and make camp," Elenna said. "We're going to get soaked."

Tom scanned the next hill and spotted an outcrop of rock that would provide shelter for the night. They began to climb towards it.

Just then Silver started to growl and his fur stood on end.

"What is it, boy?" Tom jumped off Storm and crouched beside the wolf. He looked all around but the hillside was deserted.

Elenna shivered, and Storm pranced nervously, his ears pricked up.

Then, suddenly, the horse halted, planting all four hooves firmly on the ground.

"Come on, Storm," Elenna said, touching her heels to his sides. "It's all right..." She stopped with a gasp.

Storm was slowly moving backwards down the hillside – even though he was standing still!

"Tom!" Elenna cried, as Storm started to slide more quickly. "The ground's not safe!"

"Jump off!" Tom yelled.

Storm fought to keep his balance but his hind legs slipped from under him. With Elenna clinging to his

mane, the horse fell heavily onto his side. His hooves sent great clods of mud flying into the air, and Elenna crashed to the ground with a cry.

"Storm! Elenna!" Tom shouted, his voice filled with panic.

Elenna's eyes were wide with fear as she pointed up the hill, past Tom.

"Mudslide!" she screamed.

CHAPTER TWO

SWEPT AWAY

Tom spun round. A sludgy torrent of mud was surging down the hill towards them. It looked as if the ground was *melting*.

With a terrified snort, Storm struggled to his feet, his coat caked with mud. Silver tugged at Elenna's sleeve, trying to drag her to safety. As Tom started to make his way back down the hill to them, the ground gave way beneath him. He cried out as he was sucked into the thick, swirling muck and swept down the hillside, his back scraping over tree roots as he went.

Tom saw Elenna gasp as the mass of dark mud he was caught in rushed towards her. When the mudslide hit Elenna, she reached for Tom's hand. She caught hold of it for a moment, but it was soon wrenched away. Tom reached out for her again but his fingers closed on grass and mud.

"Elenna!" he yelled.

Storm kicked wildly as he tried to escape the mudslide. Tom threw himself to one side to avoid the horse's thrashing hooves. Silver leapt to the other side of the hill. Elenna's head disappeared under the mud.

"I can't breathe!" she yelled, fighting her way to the surface.

"Reach out to your right!" Tom shouted. "Grab hold of Storm's reins!"

Blindly, Elenna reached out and managed to catch hold of the trailing leather.

As the waves of mud tossed Tom around, he caught a glimpse of the hillside above them. The entire top half was collapsing. Trees and bushes were being torn furiously from the ground, and tumbling into the mud.

We'll be buried alive! Tom thought.

He reached out for something solid to grab. His hand scraped against a boulder and he managed to find a fingerhold. He fought to hang on to the wet rock, as mud and debris rushed past him. He wasn't sure how long he could keep his grip.

Storm swept past, dragging Elenna behind him as she clung to his reins. Then the horse slammed into a group of tall, sturdy trees, and Elenna crashed into him.

"Don't let go of Storm's reins, Elenna!" Tom shouted above the roar. He saw that Elenna was holding on with all her might. Snorting with fear, Storm struggled to haul himself upright, leaning heavily against the trees.

Desperately, Tom tried to pull himself up the side of the boulder. He was exhausted, but he had to keep trying! The ground was shaking, the black mud was sucking at his ankles, but, using all his strength, he kept pulling himself up. Just a little further…

But he wasn't quick enough. With Elenna's screams echoing in his ears, Tom braced himself as another surge of mud hit him.

He was almost ripped from the boulder by the force of it. It was all he could do to drag breath into his lungs as the heavy wave of mud and debris roared past, tearing at his clothes and grazing his skin.

With a final burst of strength Tom reached for the top of the boulder. He let out a loud yell as he clawed his way to the top. His voice echoed above the angry churning of the mud. He wasn't going to be defeated!

But the mud kept coming, pulling

fiercely at Tom's legs. He could hear his knuckles popping as he strained to keep his grip on the slippery boulder. He thrashed his legs, and found a foothold just to his right. He wedged his foot into it, taking the strain off his fingers.

Taking a breath, Tom clambered back onto the top of the boulder. His tired muscles trembled as he watched the mudslide gradually become a slow ooze.

Once he was sure the danger was over, he eased himself down to the soggy ground and looked for Elenna. The hillside was destroyed. Only a few trees were left standing in the muddy wasteland. He wiped the mud from his eyes.

"Tom!" Elenna yelled. She was by the trees, waist-deep in mud and still holding tightly to Storm's reins.

Tom made his way over as they struggled to free themselves. From the other side of the hill, Silver padded across the mud to join them.

Tom was exhausted. It felt as if he were wearing a suit of armour – every small movement took enormous effort. Shivering with cold, he wrapped his arms round Storm's neck, sinking his hands into the horse's thick, muddy mane.

"I was so scared," said Elenna, hugging Tom tight. "I thought we were going to die."

"Me too," gasped Tom. His legs felt wobbly.

"You're freezing," said Elenna.

Tom saw that Elenna was shivering too and her face was pale. This wasn't the time to show weakness. He had to be strong. "I'm all right," he said. "I'll soon warm up once we get moving."

Elenna nodded. "Good idea. Let's get to safer ground and then make camp."

The four of them hiked towards the rocky outcrop Tom had spotted earlier. The rain had stopped, but the ground was still thick with mud. They made their way up painfully and slowly.

By the time they reached the rocks, the sun had set. The air had grown colder and it was now too dark to see. Guided by starlight, Tom and Elenna found a cave in the outcrop.

"Let's make camp in here," Tom suggested. He could tell from the look on Elenna's face that she was scared.

"What if there's another mudslide?" she asked. "We could be trapped inside."

Tom knew they didn't have a choice. It was too cold and dangerous to spend the night without some

shelter. They would have to take
their chances.

They stepped into the cave. It
smelled damp and echoed with their
footsteps. As they lay down on some
dry leaves, Tom wished they could

have a warm fire. His stomach was growling with hunger, too. But before he could suggest they build a fire or cook some dinner, he fell asleep.

CHAPTER THREE

IN THE SHADOW OF THE MOUNTAINS

Tom and Elenna woke late. The sun was already shining brightly into the mouth of the cave. Every muscle in Tom's body ached. Rubbing the sleep from his eyes, he gazed in amazement at the cave walls. They were covered with ancient drawings. It had been too dark and he had been too tired to notice them the night before.

The drawings had been made with charcoal and seemed to be telling a story. Tom recognised the five jagged mountains and simple pictures of men with spears and clubs. In one picture an enormous hand held the mountains in its palm, and men were looking up at it in awe.

Elenna woke as he was studying the drawings. "What are they?" she asked.

"I don't know," said Tom. "But they're very old. And it looks as if someone knew about Arcta the mountain giant a long time ago."

"It's late. We should get moving," Elenna said, standing up.

"All right," Tom agreed, tearing his eyes away from the drawings. He took hold of Storm's reins and followed Elenna to the mouth of the cave.

They stood blinking in the sunlight. The mudslide had left a thick scar on the landscape, blocking the main mountain road. To get round it, they would have to follow the muddy scar down into the next valley, then climb back up to the road.

Tom and Elenna walked beside Storm with Silver at their heels. It was a steep journey down into the valley, with a sheer cliff on one side. The ground was covered in mud, pebbles and rubble, and Tom and Elenna had to pick their way carefully, their feet slipping and sliding. One wrong step and it would be a very long fall.

When they reached the bottom of the valley, Tom looked at his map. Then he gazed around. "This is strange," he said. "We're in a valley surrounded by five peaks and the glowing path ends here. We should have reached the town by now. But it's nowhere to be seen."

They walked on. Then, suddenly, a loud crack rang out from beneath Storm's hooves.

"What was *that*?" Tom asked, crouching down. He quickly cleared away some of the dust. His hands scraped against something. It was a piece of slate, neatly overlapped by others.

"Roof tiles," he said, then realised where they were. "Elenna, we're standing on a roof!"

Elenna looked up at the bare rock face above them, which was crisscrossed by a web of cracks. "This is a house buried by a landslide," she cried. "The mountain could collapse any minute!"

"Look," said Tom, pointing to a shape further up the valley. It was the top of an archway. "I think there's a whole street buried under this rubble!"

Using the archway as a guide, they worked out where the street must have been. Then they made their way over the rubble. Beyond the archway, they found a part of town built into the mountainside. The landslide hadn't buried these buildings. The houses were grand and tall with wooden fronts, and the street in front of them was neatly lined with cobblestones. But the place seemed deserted.

"I hope everyone managed to get to safety," said Elenna.

Silver sniffed the air. He growled uneasily and looked towards the jagged mountain peaks.

"What's wrong, boy?" Elenna held him by the scruff of his neck, but he strained against her grip. Silver never disobeyed Elenna. She frowned and pointed at the cobbled street. "We're going *this* way." She looked at Tom. "What's wrong with him?"

But as she spoke, shouts came from further down the street.

"*Stop, thieves!*" someone yelled.

Tom jumped onto Storm, and Elenna leapt up behind him. He drew his sword and pressed his heels against the horse's sides.

Storm didn't need telling twice. He

bolted along the cobbled street towards the sound of trouble.

"Silver isn't following us!" Elenna cried.

The wolf stood motionless, still staring towards the mountains.

"We'll go back for him," Tom told her. Storm thundered over the cobblestones, making it difficult for them to hold on. "Right now, someone needs our help."

They turned into a narrow back alley. Three men, sacks slung over their

shoulders, were blocking the way.

"Whoa, Storm." Tom eased his horse to a standstill. "What's happening here?"

The tallest man noticed Tom's sword and smiled. "Well, well. A bold little knight."

An old man came puffing and panting round the corner, pointing a finger at the three men. "Don't let them pass!" he cried, leaning heavily against the wall of a house as he caught his breath. "They're robbing food from people's houses!"

"What else can we do?" snapped a small, fat man, shifting the heavy sack on his shoulder. "We have families to feed."

"This month's supplies never came — you know that!" added the thin man next to him. "We need *something* to eat."

"But those things are not yours to take!" said the old man sternly.

The three men looked at one another. Their expressions hardened.

Tom looked at the thieves and saw desperation in their faces. They didn't look dishonest. Thanks to Malvel's curse, good people were stealing in order to survive.

Then the tallest man bunched his fists and turned back to Tom. "Get out of our way, boy," he said. "Or you'll live to regret it!"

CHAPTER FOUR

BURIED ALIVE

Tom jumped down from Storm, holding his sword out in front of him, tensing himself for a fight. Elenna leapt beside him, readying her bow.

Then a sudden growling made Tom turn. It was Silver! The wolf bared his teeth as he stalked towards the thieves, his fur bristling. Even Tom felt a moment of awe when he saw Silver's glistening fangs.

"A wolf!" cried the short man. "It must have come down from the mountains."

Silver crept towards the men, narrowing his eyes and snarling deep in his throat.

The short man dropped his sack and took to his heels, followed by the thin man. The tallest man's eyes grew wide with fear, then he fled with the others, his stolen loot scattering behind him as he ran.

The old man leaned against a wall. He was trembling.

"The wolf won't hurt you," Tom told him. "He's with us. Are you all right?"

"I'll be fine," gasped the old man. "Thank you for your help. I am Belco, mayor of the town."

Just then, in the distance, they heard a loud crash followed by blood-curdling screams.

"Another landslide!" Belco cried.

"Come on!" said Tom. He helped
the old man onto Storm, then
jumped up in front of him. Once
more Tom kicked his heels into
Storm's side and they sped towards
the sound of the crash. Elenna and
Silver followed them at a run.

As they turned into another street,
Tom brought Storm to a halt. A group
of townspeople stood before a house
that was crushed under a mound of
rocks. From inside the house, they
could hear muffled cries for help.

"What happened?" Belco asked
a woman in the crowd.

"Rocks fell onto the house from the
mountain," the woman replied. "Those
three thieves are trapped inside."

"Serves them right," said another.

"Aye, they ought to be left in there

to die!" called out a man.

Others muttered in agreement.

Tom listened to the angry crowd. He had to do something.

"No!" he yelled. Everyone turned to look at him. "We must save these men. It is our duty as citizens of Avantia to help those in need."

Elenna and Silver stepped up beside him, and slowly the crowd began to nod as they began to agree with what Tom was saying.

There was a loud groan as the frame of the house buckled under the weight of the stone. They would have to hurry and free the men before the house collapsed altogether.

"Help us!" came a muffled voice from inside.

"Don't worry!" Tom shouted. "We're going to get you out!"

A sudden screech of anger echoed

down from the mountains like a gust
of icy wind.

"What was that?" gasped Belco.

"Arcta!" Tom said to himself.

Then his heart jumped at the sound
of heavy footsteps clattering on the
cobbles. Eight burly men appeared
round the street corner and stepped
towards him.

CHAPTER FIVE

DANGER ON THE MOUNTAIN

Tom gripped his sword.

"We're here to help," the biggest man said.

Relief swept over Tom. Turning towards the house, he began to think how they could free the three thieves.

"We need to know where the door is so we can remove the rocks from the front of it!" Tom yelled to the trapped men. "Can you bang on it for us?"

A faint thumping started up.

The eight men wasted no time. They braced their shoulders against the rocks and started to heave them out of the way. But some of the rocks were huge. Even when the men used wooden poles as levers, they were impossible to shift.

One man looked up grimly, his hair wet with sweat. "It will take all night to clear this."

"The house could collapse before then!" Tom said, desperately. There had to be some other way.

Then he remembered something he had learned from his uncle the blacksmith: everything has a breaking point. One day his uncle had demonstrated this by shattering a

sheet of metal with a soft tap of a
hammer. He had explained that it was
just a matter of finding the point of
weakness, then applying pressure to it.

Tom studied the largest boulder
closely. He didn't know what he was
looking for until he saw it – a small
crack near the bottom. But it wasn't
a crack, just a line where two
different types of rock met.

Tom pulled his sword out of its
scabbard and held it up in front of
him. Crouching down, he brought
the sword back, keeping his eyes
focused on the small line. With all
his strength, Tom swung the sword,
striking just to the left of the line.
The impact sent painful vibrations up
his arms, but nothing happened to
the rock. Tom took aim again and
swung the sword even harder.

This time, the blow hit the line.

There was a sharp cracking sound and the rock crumbled into pieces. Tom could hear gasps of shock from the men behind him.

"What is that sword made of?" someone asked.

"Never mind that," said Tom, examining the next boulder for its weak spot. "We should clear this rubble."

The men scrambled to drag away the smaller pieces of rock. Tom kept bringing his sword down in ringing blows against the massive boulders. The muscles in his arms were soon trembling with the effort, but he couldn't stop. Not while people were still trapped in the house.

With a surge of hope Tom saw the door to the house slowly being revealed. He fell to his knees and used his bare hands to dig away the

last of the rubble.

Finally the door creaked open and the three thieves staggered out, coughing and spluttering.

"Thank you!" they cried.

The tallest thief shook Tom's hand. "I owe you my life," he said. "My name is Randall."

Belco smiled at Tom. "I don't know

where you learned to use a sword so well, but that was quick-thinking, my young friend." He clapped his hands and turned to the crowd. "Let's forgive these men – I think they have learned their lesson. And we must accompany our new guests to the town hall." To Tom and Elenna he said, "Most of the townspeople are already sheltering there. Come along."

"Thanks, but we'll have to join you later," Tom called, hanging back with Elenna. "We have something to do." He said to Elenna in a low voice, "We can't lose any more time. We must find Arcta the mountain giant and stop him before he can cause another landslide – or kill someone."

She nodded. "Let's go."

Tom felt a tap on his shoulder. It was Randall. "Are you going up the mountain?" he said worriedly.

Tom and Elenna looked at each other but said nothing.

"You do know about Arcta, don't you?" he continued.

Elenna glanced at Tom, uneasily. "Everyone knows the old stories. Arcta is one of the Beasts," she said.

"But...do you believe he's real?" asked Randall.

Tom nodded. "Yes, we do."

"Can you tell us where to find him?" asked Elenna.

Randall sighed. "Well, the town legend is that he lives somewhere called the Place of the Eagles. All the short cuts are buried, but the main trail will take you there. It splits in five directions – always take the right-hand path. Then an hour's hike will bring you to a rocky plateau. According to stories, that is where you will find the Beast."

"Thanks," said Tom.

"Be careful…" Randall warned.

Tom and Elenna climbed onto Storm. With a snort, the horse cantered towards the mountains, steam puffing from his nostrils.

Tom was both afraid and excited as they set off up the winding trail. Looking up at the towering peaks, it was incredible to think how small they had looked in the distance. The mountains seemed to stretch as high as the stars, their summits lost in dark wisps of cloud.

The trail twisted and turned up the mountainside, but Storm kept his footing. Sheer rock faces rose up to their right, and to their left cliffs dropped into nothingness. The higher they climbed, the colder the air became. It was harder to breathe, too.

Finally, the trail levelled out onto a plain, where five paths led in different directions. It was eerily quiet.

Tom pointed. "Randall said always to take the right-hand path..."

Elenna frowned. "But it looks as if Silver wants to take the left."

The wolf was edging along the left-hand path with his head cocked to one side, as if listening to something. Then he started barking loudly.

"What's got into you, Silver?" Elenna asked in surprise.

Suddenly the wolf bolted down the left-hand path.

"He must want us to follow him," said Tom. "Maybe he knows where Arcta is!"

At a touch of Tom's heels, Storm

galloped after the wolf. Tom and
Elenna leaned forward to take as
much of their weight off the horse's
back as possible. Storm was brave
and strong, but it was hard work for
him on these steep mountain paths.

Then Elenna looked up ahead and
gasped. "Silver, come back!" she
yelled. "Now!"

"What is it?" said Tom.

She pointed. "Look!"

Tom felt a chill go through him, colder than ice. It looked as if a dark cloud was rolling down the mountainside towards them. Then the ground started to shake. Tom could feel the vibrations travelling up his legs. It was like nothing he'd ever felt before.

Tom knew that was no cloud.

It was a landslide.

CHAPTER SIX

THE COMING OF
THE BEAST

For a second, Tom hesitated. They
might just be able to get out of the
way of the landslide, but it would
mean leaving Silver, who was by
now far ahead of them on the path.
Before Tom could make a decision,
Elenna leapt to the ground.

"There's Silver!" she shouted,
pointing as a grey-white figure

darted into the mouth of a small cave, half-hidden in the mountainside. "Silver!" she yelled above the gathering roar of the landslide. "I have to get him," she cried, running towards the wolf.

Tom looked up and saw enormous rocks and piles of debris hurtling down the mountainside towards

them. Silver barked wildly, running back and forth into the cave. The landslide was almost on top of them!

Elenna reached Silver as the first pieces of rock rained down. Storm reared up, his hooves kicking the air.

"We've got to get out of the way!" Tom cried. "Or we're going to be buried alive!"

Tom brought Storm under control and turned him round. He didn't want to abandon Elenna and the wolf, but if he escaped the landslide he could return for them when it was over.

Leaning forward in the saddle, he urged the horse into a gallop back

down the mountainside. Rocks flew through the air around them.

"Faster, Storm!" Tom urged. "Come on—" He broke off with a cry of pain as a chunk of rock cracked into his shoulder and knocked him off the horse. He felt himself tumbling and tried to throw his hands out in front of him to break his fall, but it was too late. He hit the path with a bone-jarring thud. The pain washed over him, and he could feel himself blacking out. "I have to stay awake," he muttered, forcing his eyes open. But his vision was blurry. He heard the clatter of Storm's hooves disappear into the roar. Without thinking, he rolled over into a small ditch next to the path.

Then the tidal wave of rubble, shingle and rocks poured past him. His mouth and eyes filled with grit.

He squeezed them shut.

Soon, everything became quiet again. For long, silent seconds he didn't dare to open his eyes. When he did, the world was dark and he was covered with dust and silt thrown up by the rocks that had hurtled past.

Gasping for air, he looked over and saw that Storm was buried up to his chest in silt, waiting patiently to be freed. But where were Elenna and Silver?

"Elenna! Silver!" he called out, straining to hear a response. After a few long, anxious moments, he heard the muffled sound of barking from the cave further up the mountain. Then he saw that the cave's entrance had been completely blocked by the landslide.

Tom climbed back up to the cave.

"Elenna!"

He could just hear her cries for help. He began to scrape away some of the tightly packed dirt.

"Tom! We're trapped!" Elenna called faintly. "We're all right for now, but we'll soon run out of air!"

Tom looked round, his mind racing. He had to free his friends. He began digging wildly at the silt and rubble that was blocking the cave, when, all of a sudden, he hit something solid – a boulder.

"Elenna, hold on," Tom called. "I'm working as fast as I can—"

He broke off as a pounding thump shook through the ground, soon followed by another and another, each one growing louder and becoming closer.

"Footsteps!" he gasped.

Tom turned.

An enormous, terrifying figure appeared round a bend in the mountain path, feeling his way. He paused and gave a terrifying, ground-shaking roar. The whole mountain trembled.

Arcta the Mountain Giant was as tall as the highest trees, with a body almost as wide. His arms and legs bulged with muscle, and his feet left huge indentations in the ground. His gnarled hands ended in yellow claws and his mouth gaped open to reveal crooked, brown teeth. Unlike the Beasts Tom had already freed – the fire dragon and the sea serpent – there was no enchanted golden collar around his neck. Instead a black blindfold covered the Beast's eyes, held in place by a glowing knot. This was Malvel's curse. The Beast must be driven mad by the loss of his sight.

But despite his pity, Tom felt fear rising up inside him, pushing the air from his throat.

"Tom!" Elenna yelled. "What's going on out there?"

"Sshh!" Tom hissed desperately.

But it was too late. At the sound of Elenna's voice, the mountain giant stiffened. He swung his head slowly in Tom's direction. Then, with another thundering roar, he lumbered towards the cave.

CHAPTER SEVEN

A RACE AGAINST TIME

The giant took another crashing step towards Tom. Then he stopped and sniffed the air.

Tom dropped to the ground. He realised that the dirt and silt that had covered him during the landslide was helping to hide his scent. He tried to breathe as quietly as possible so Arcta wouldn't hear him. But there was no way to tell Elenna and Silver inside the cave that they had to be quiet, too.

Silver let out a growl that could be heard even through the blocked cave. Arcta turned at the sound and took another thunderous step closer. Tom didn't dare move. He was now right underneath the giant and his eyes were level with Arcta's feet. The rough yellow toenails were thick with grime. If Arcta took another step, Tom would be crushed. He tried to keep his breathing shallow and quiet, but he could feel his body shaking with tension. He clamped his mouth shut and hoped that his teeth wouldn't start chattering. Arcta swung a heavy fist and let out a roar of frustration.

Then he turned and began to grope his way back up the mountain. Tom

felt a rush of relief. The giant had given up!

But just when he thought he was safe, Silver growled again – more loudly this time. Arcta snapped his head back round. He let out another gigantic bellow and stomped furiously back towards the cave. Tom had no choice. He had to distract the mountain giant to save Elenna and Silver. He had to run – and hope Arcta would hear him and follow. Otherwise the giant would smash the entrance to the cave and find his friends! Even with the blindfold, he would be able to hear and smell them as they tried to escape.

Tom took off back down the mountain path, running as fast as he could. As he passed Storm – who was still buried up to his middle – he grabbed the rope the trader had given him, then veered off the path into the pine trees. He thought quickly. "Somehow I've got to climb higher than Arcta," he said to himself, "so I'm level with his head. Then maybe I can undo the knot of that enchanted blindfold."

Weaving through the trees, Tom could hear Arcta coming after him. Each footstep shook the ground. Tom could hear trees snapping and crashing as the giant knocked them out of his way.

There was no way Tom could outrun the giant – even with the blindfold he was too big and too fast. Now that he had brought him away from the cave, Tom had to find a way to lose him.

Scrambling down a slope, Tom spotted a patch of blueberry bushes. He made a quick left into them, and, as he came out on the other side, he saw a huge tree with a hollow in the base of its trunk. Tom dived inside, into the rough, damp blackness.

The old tree shook with each pounding step of the giant. Again Tom tried to calm his breathing and be as still as possible.

A tremendous roar echoed in Tom's ears, and then all was quiet. Tom waited a few seconds before peering from his hiding spot.

Just a few short yards away, Tom could see the giant's massive legs standing as still as if they were the trunks of trees. Now was his chance. If he could climb to the top of the tree, he might be able to lure Arcta close enough to free him.

But before Tom had a chance to scale the tree, Arcta began moving away. Tom listened as the sound of the giant's footsteps disappeared into the distance.

He had to hurry. Elenna and Silver would be running out of air soon, but he knew there was no way he could save them if Arcta was still on the loose. He had to free the Beast first. Then he could come back for his friends. Tom moved nimbly and quietly, following the thump of Arcta's giant footsteps.

It was hard work climbing the mountain. With each footstep, loose rocks and pebbles would shift under him, threatening his balance. But he kept climbing, until he reached a narrow ridge. Clinging to cracks in the rock, he followed it as it snaked upwards into the clouds.

Soon he emerged onto a rocky plateau. Looking down, Tom spotted the giant. He was resting just beneath him on a narrow ledge, his huge head in his hands. Below him was a vast, misty abyss. Tom shivered. Above, a bird gave a harsh cry. Tom glanced up. It was an eagle circling on the currents of air. *This must be the Place of the Eagles*, he thought.

Tom lay down flat on the plateau. The stone was hard and cold. He could see the glowing knot that held the blindfold in place. It looked like

a beautiful black flower. If he edged forward he might just be able to reach the knot and untie it.

But he had to hurry. Elenna and Silver could be suffocating.

Heart pounding, he edged forward until his arms reached the knot. His fingers tingled as they touched the shimmering dark fabric. He pulled very gently.

Come on! he silently begged the knot. He felt it loosen slightly, but

knew he had to be quick.

Starting to panic, he pulled a little harder.

Too hard.

Arcta suddenly sensed him. With a furious roar, he swung round and lashed out with his huge, clawed hand. It smashed against the side of the mountain, close to where Tom

lay. The impact echoed around the mountains. Tom clung to the plateau.

But to his horror, he saw that a crack had appeared in the rock beneath him. Tom could only watch as the crack zig-zagged its way through the rock and the ledge below. With a groan, the split widened and the rocks started to

crumble apart, dirt and pebbles raining down. Any second now the entire rock face would give way, and Tom would plunge to his death.

Realising he had no choice, Tom took a deep breath. "While there's blood in my veins, I'll free this Beast!" he cried. Then he scrambled to his feet and jumped through the air towards the giant. He just managed to grab hold of the blindfold.

The giant roared, and sprang to his feet. Tom swung through the air but somehow kept his grip. Arcta swatted at his head with his enormous hands, trying to get at Tom. Tom twisted this way and that, trying to avoid the blows. If so much as a finger landed on him, he would be squashed flat. But he couldn't let go – if he did, he would fall into the abyss.

Enraged, the giant staggered about, trying to regain his balance. The ledge they were on was narrow, and Tom saw Arcta was blundering towards the edge.

Suddenly, with a thunderclap of splitting rock, the ledge gave way.

Arcta and Tom plunged together into empty space.

CHAPTER EIGHT

OVER THE EDGE

The world rushed by, as Tom clung to the giant. For a few seconds they were in freefall.

Then they landed with a hard thump on another, even smaller ledge. Tom felt relief flood through him. But they were falling so fast that they skidded straight across the smooth rock. Without time to stop, they went over the edge and were falling again.

The giant tried to thrust his gnarled
fingers into cracks and holes in the
mountainside. But he couldn't stop
them from tumbling towards the
misty chasm. Arcta roared and threw
back his head.

Tom was shaken free. His fingers
closed round thin air as his hands were
torn away from the blindfold. He
hurtled through the air and fell heavily
on a steep rocky slope, scrabbling for
a handhold. His fingertips dug into
a crack in the rock. Terror swept
through him as he glanced down. The
abyss was waiting to swallow him.

To his left, he saw that Arcta had managed to cling on to the rocky slope, too. But now they were both hanging helplessly.

Tom looked up. He was only an arm's length from a path. But he was barely managing to hold on. His fingers were already numb, his arms tingling fiercely with pins and needles.

Swinging his feet, Tom found a foothold. Then, with the last of his strength, he dragged himself up onto the path and lay there gasping.

Time was running out. He had to get to Elenna and Silver before it was too late. But he still had to free Arcta. There might not be another chance. "I will not fail Avantia," he said to himself.

Tom peered down. The giant's fingers were wedged into a crevice just below the path, his massive body disappearing into the mist below. Without his sight he was helpless.

If Tom was going to free the Beast, now was the time. He crept on his hands and knees to where the giant's fingers gripped the rock. He realised he was going to have to climb down Arcta's arm in order to reach the knot.

Taking a deep breath, Tom took the rope that the trader had given him and tied one end round a tree root sticking out of the cliff face. He then tied the other end round his waist. It was now or never.

Slowly, Tom climbed onto the giant's hand and began to slide carefully down Arcta's enormous arm. The Beast let out a ferocious roar. But Tom was safe. So long as Arcta was clinging to the rock, he wouldn't be able to swat at Tom.

Trying not to look into the deadly

abyss, Tom held his breath and inched his way down until he reached Arcta's massive shoulders. Then he scrambled onto the back of the giant's neck. Holding onto the enchanted blindfold with one hand, Tom reached for the knot with the other. He took another deep breath as he pulled firmly at the black knot.

This time the fabric gave as if it were made of the lightest cobweb. The blindfold vanished in a bloom of coloured light. Arcta the Mountain Giant was free!

CHAPTER NINE

NEW BEGINNINGS

As the blindfold disappeared, Arcta let out a roar of relief. Tom fell towards the misty depths – and was saved by the rope tied round his waist.

But they were both still dangling above the misty chasm. Arcta raised his head and looked up. Tom gasped when he saw the giant had only one eye instead of two, right in the centre of his forehead. It was deep brown, the colour of the rocks around him.

Tom could see a small ledge just to the left of the giant. He didn't know if the Beast would understand, but he pointed to it.

Amazingly, Arcta moved his foot to the ledge. With something to stand on, he was able to raise himself up onto the path above. With a great struggle, the giant pulled himself to safety.

Tom sighed with relief. He had succeeded in his mission. Another Beast had been set free from Malvel's evil magic.

His relief didn't last long. With a lurch of his stomach, he remembered Elenna and Silver. He had to get them out of the cave – and soon.

Then Tom felt the rope around his waist tighten. Someone was pulling him to safety.

With a final jolt, Tom found himself on the path – at the giant, clawed feet of Arcta! Looking up, he saw a gentle expression on the Beast's face. Tom wanted to say thank you, but there was no time.

Scrambling to his feet, he called up, "I need your help!"

The Beast let out a booming snort.

"I need to rescue my friends," Tom cried, pointing towards the pile of rocks covering Elenna and Silver. "They're trapped in the cave where you first found me."

Without a moment's hesitation, the Beast scooped Tom up in his hand and swiftly made his way down the steep path, his footing sure now that his sight had been returned to him.

In an instant, Arcta's enormous strides had brought them back to the cave.

Storm was standing next to the pile of boulders blocking the cave, pawing anxiously at the ground. He must have freed himself while Tom was struggling with the giant.

"In there," Tom called out, pointing to the blocked entrance. "They're in there."

Arcta set Tom down, and, with one movement of his massive fist, cleared the rocks and debris from the front of the cave. Tom tried to peer in, but couldn't see through the heavy dust that hung in the air.

Then, in a leaping bound, Silver burst from the entrance.

"Silver!" Tom shouted. "Where's Elenna?"

"Here. Over here." Elenna's voice was faint.

Tom rushed into the cave. His friend was slumped in a corner. Her face was pale-blue and she looked very tired, but she was still breathing. She was alive!

Carrying her in his arms, Tom brought her out of the cave into the sunlight and fresh mountain air.

"You did it, Tom. You really did it," Elenna gasped as she looked up at the towering giant. She paused. "You know, he doesn't look so bad, after all."

Tom thought about the heart-pounding chase through the pine forest, the terrifying fall from the cliff, and the dangerous move along Arcta's arm to untie the enchanted blindfold.

"No, not so bad at all," he said with a smile. He had survived another chapter of the Beast Quest!

As Tom set Elenna on the ground, a beautiful golden-brown feather floated down and landed at his feet.

He bent down and picked it up. It was an eagle's feather. He looked up at Arcta. The giant bared his brown teeth in a kindly smile.

After his battles with Ferno the Fire Dragon and Sepron the Sea Serpent, Tom knew exactly what to do with the gift. Grabbing his shield, he placed the feather at the top. As if it were a key to a lock, it sank right into the shield and was sealed there, along with Ferno's scale and Sepron's tooth. He ran his fingers over the surface. It was smooth again.

With a final snort, the giant raised a clawed hand in farewell and lumbered back into the mountains.

Just then, three little wolf cubs came tumbling out of the cave! Their coats were white, with little smudges of grey around their pricked-up ears and tiny feet.

"I found them in the cave," Elenna said. "This was why Silver ran off in the first place. I knew there had to be a reason he'd disobeyed me!"

"He must have sensed they were in danger," Tom agreed.

"Not any more," said Elenna, pointing back down the mountain trail to where a pure white wolf was hovering. "Look – that must be the mother!"

The cubs bounded towards her. They all watched as the mother cuffed and licked them.

"She must have lost them in one of the landslides," said Elenna, stroking Silver behind the ear. He howled at the mother, who yapped twice, before nudging her cubs back down the mountain path.

"We did it!" cried Tom. Now that the danger was over he felt full of energy and excitement.

"We did!" agreed Elenna.

They grabbed each other's hands and swung round and round, before noticing that another figure had gradually appeared before them in the mouth of the cave. They stumbled dizzily to a halt.

"Wizard Aduro!" Tom breathed. He knew it was only a magical image that Aduro had sent, but it still felt good to see his twinkling blue eyes.

"Greetings, my young friends," Aduro said, smiling fondly. "I have been watching your progress from the king's castle."

"We've freed the third Beast," Tom told him proudly.

"I am aware of that!" said the wizard. "Congratulations! Your bravery is saving the whole kingdom."

Tom's face looked sad for a moment.

"I just wish my father could see me now. I hope he would be proud of me."

"I'm sure he would, Tom," said the wizard kindly, then he added, "Your aunt and uncle know you are on an important mission for the king – *they* are proud. And I see Arcta has given you an enchanted eagle's feather for your shield. Just like the dragon's scale and the serpent's tooth, it will give you magical protection. Should you ever find yourself falling from a great height, hold the shield above your head and it will slow your fall."

Tom looked at Elenna and grinned. "Fantastic!"

"You have done well," Aduro told them. "But the greatest dangers still lie ahead. Will you continue with your Quest?"

Storm chose that moment to

whinny, and Silver barked in response. Elenna beamed.

Tom nodded firmly. "We will."

Aduro smiled. "Then you must travel further south to the shadowy plains," he told them. "It is where the cattle roam. Another cursed Beast awaits you there – Tagus the Horse-man. Until he was trapped by Malvel's evil spell, he protected the herds of cattle that provide food for all of Avantia. Now he is attacking and killing what he used to defend."

"We will find him," said Tom.

"Good luck," said the wizard. "But first you must tell Belco the mayor that the town here is safe, and that the people can begin to trade again."

"We will," promised Tom and Elenna.

Then the wizard raised his hand in a salute, and slowly his magical image faded to nothing in the thin mountain air. He was gone.

Tom and Elenna stood silently for a moment, Silver and Storm at their sides, thinking about the next stage of the Beast Quest. Then Elenna turned to Tom, and he grinned at her.

Whatever dangers lay ahead, they would face them together.

Join Tom on the next stage
of the Beast Quest

Meet

TAGUS
THE HORSE-MAN

Can Tom free Tagus from
Malvel's evil spell?

PROLOGUE

Victor woke with a start. Grabbing his sword, he sat up and looked round wildly. It was just before dawn and the sky was beginning to lighten in the east. The coals from last night's campfire were still glowing. Victor surveyed the shadowy plains and the herd of cattle. Nothing seemed out of the ordinary.

"Must have been a bad dream," he thought, and settled back onto his bedroll.

But he couldn't sleep. In the last week, there had been three attacks on cattle during the night. In the last attack, four calves had been killed. No one knew who or what was responsible. Victor wasn't sure what to think, but he was certainly glad the night was almost over. He only had to keep watch over the herd until the morning. The men were all asleep beside their own campfires, away from the cattle.

He listened to the sounds of the plains. There was a slight breeze rustling the tall grasses and he could hear the last of the crickets chirping softly. Then a bird called out over the lowing cattle.

Wait a minute…that wasn't right. The cattle should be sleeping, not lowing!

Sitting up, Victor looked closely at his herd. The cattle were huddled together more tightly than usual, with their calves grouped in the centre – a sign that they felt threatened. But why?

Just then Victor heard the sound of hooves drumming in the distance. Was it just his imagination?

The cattle began to stamp restlessly. Victor leapt to his feet. The hoofbeats were growing closer!

Something was out there.

Then a large shape loomed out of the darkness in front of him. Suddenly, standing before him in the red glow of the campfire was a horrifying Beast.

Victor gasped. The monster had the torso of a giant man, but it was attached to the body of a powerful stallion!

Stumbling back in terror, Victor stared up at the creature. His dark hair and beard were wildly tangled, and the reflection from the campfire had turned his black eyes a flaming, angry red.

The Beast reared up on its hind legs, grunting fiercely, its hooves pounding the air. With a sense of panic, Victor realised it was going to charge!

He tried to dive out of the way. But he wasn't fast enough. One of the Beast's hooves struck him on the head, knocking him to the ground. Then the Beast galloped through the fire, scattering the red-hot coals in a flurry of sparks. It flung its head back and roared as the dry grass of the plains began to catch fire.

Dazed, Victor saw the creature charge towards the helpless, frantic cattle...

Then the pain overcame him and everything went black.

CHAPTER ONE

A THOUSAND HOOVES

"I think that was the biggest challenge yet," said Tom.

He sat tall in his saddle as he rode from the northern mountains of Avantia on his black horse, Storm. His friend Elenna sat behind him as she usually did, her arms around his waist. Tom had just freed Arcta the mountain giant from the evil spell of Malvel the Dark Wizard, and they were all tired. But Storm bravely pressed on, with Silver, Elenna's tame wolf, padding quietly after them. It was mid-afternoon and the sun was strong.

"I thought I'd be trapped in that cave for ever," Elenna agreed. "Arcta was so angry!"

"I'd be angry too if an evil wizard had enslaved me!" Tom said. He gave a sigh of satisfaction. "But Arcta is free now. There will be no more trouble."

"Not from him," Elenna pointed out. "But we have a new Beast Quest now. How long do you think it will take to reach the central plains?"

"Not long," said Tom. "I just hope we're ready for the next test." He reached out and touched the hilt of his sword, and was reminded of the challenges he had faced so far: Ferno the fire dragon, Sepron the sea serpent, Arcta the mountain giant... Once more he thought about his father, Taladon the Swift, and wondered if he would be proud of what he had achieved on this Quest. He hoped so. His father had disappeared when Tom was a baby, but somehow he felt he knew him.

"While there is blood in my veins," he thought, "I will not let my father down!" Then he remembered that King Hugo and his adviser Wizard Aduro had trusted him with this Quest – he didn't want to let them down, either.

"I know you can do it," Elenna said, giving him a playful jab. "And don't forget, you've got me to protect you."

Tom glanced over his shoulder and smiled. "I haven't forgotten. I'm really glad we met! I'd never have made it this far without you."

He brought Storm to a halt and pulled out his magical map from his pocket. Elenna peered over his shoulder. A glowing red line showed the road from the mountains of the north to the central plains, which were surrounded by a ridge of hills. Tiny cattle moved about on the plains, where there was rich grass for them to eat.

"I think we're about here." Tom pointed to the edge of the hills on the map. "It can't be too far now."

He put the map away and, with a nudge of his heels, urged Storm on. "We're getting close," he said. "We should keep an eye out for the next Beast."

"Wizard Aduro said he's half-man, half-horse," Elenna said, shivering.

Tom nodded. "Tagus. He's attacking the cattle on the plains. With no cattle the people who live there will have little to eat and nothing to trade. They could starve."

"And so could the rest of the kingdom," Elenna added anxiously.

Tom tightened his grip on the reins. Storm whinnied, as if he knew what they were up against. Tom patted his horse's neck. With each Quest, their bond grew stronger.

Soon they came to the crest of a low hill. Tom reined in Storm and looked out across the wide plains, which stretched as far as he could see. He could see the long grasses swaying in the breeze. A river wound through clumps of trees. In the distance, a lake glinted in the sunlight. Silver's ears pricked up and he sniffed the air eagerly.

"It's beautiful!" Elenna exclaimed. "Maybe Wizard Aduro sent us here before Tagus had the chance to do terrible damage."

"Could be." Tom's heartbeat quickened with hope. In the south, the crops had been burned by Ferno the fire dragon. In the west, Sepron the sea serpent had flooded the coast. Arcta the mountain giant had nearly destroyed the northern mountains with landslides. Tom had almost forgotten what ordinary, peaceful countryside looked like. "Look over there," he said, pointing into the distance. He could just make out square grey towers and rooftops covered with red tiles. "That must be the town."

"Then let's go!" said Elenna.

Storm cantered down the hill towards the plains. Tom enjoyed the steady beat of his hooves, sensing his horse's rising excitement. Silver let out a joyful yelp and sprang ahead of them. He disappeared into the long grass until all Tom and Elenna could see of him was the tip of his tail.

On the breeze Tom could smell a hint of smoke, as if a campfire were burning nearby. He scanned the horizon to see if he could catch sight of it. But all he could see was a herd of cattle, moving towards them in a thick mass.

As they watched, Tom and Elenna began to sense that something was wrong.

The herd wasn't walking peacefully. They were stampeding!

"They're heading right for us!" cried Tom.

"Silver!" Elenna yelled frantically. She let out a piercing whistle, and within seconds the grey wolf was bounding through the tall grass towards them.

Tom kicked Storm's flanks once more, and the horse took off across the plains in the direction of the town, galloping as fast as he could, with Silver sprinting just behind.

But the stampeding herd was gaining on them. Dust began to fill the air, and the pounding of hooves on the hard ground was deafening.

Tom looked over his shoulder. The herd was much larger then he had thought. There must have been a thousand massive animals, each the size of a large boulder. They were charging blindly, trampling anything that stood in their way. The ground was shaking under their weight.

"Hurry, Storm!" Tom yelled above the roar of the stampede.

He bent his head into Storm's mane, and could feel Elenna gripping onto him as they flew across the plains towards the town. Suddenly Storm skidded to a stop.

"Go, Storm! Keep going!" Tom yelled. "We're almost there—"

Then he heard a crackling sound and looked up. Instantly, he knew why Storm had halted.

In front of them was a wall of fire. The dry grass of the plains had been set alight – and it was spreading swiftly.

They were trapped!

Follow this quest to the end in TAGUS THE HORSE-MAN.

Win an exclusive
Beast Quest T-shirt and goody bag!

Tom has battled many fearsome Beasts and we want to know which one is your favourite! Send us a drawing or painting of your favourite Beast and tell us in 30 words why you think it's the best.

Each month we will select **three** winners to receive a Beast Quest T-shirt and goody bag!

Send your entry on a postcard to
BEAST QUEST COMPETITION
Orchard Books, 338 Euston Road, London NW1 3BH.

Australian readers should email:
childrens.books@hachette.com.au

New Zealand readers should write to:
Beast Quest Competition, 23 O'Connell St, Auckland 1010, NZ, or email: childrensbooks@hachette.co.nz

**Don't forget to include your name and address.
Only one entry per child.**

Good luck!

Join the Quest,
Join the Tribe

www.beastquest.co.uk

Have you checked out the Beast Quest website?
It's the place to go for games, downloads, activities,
sneak previews and lots of fun!

You can read all about your favourite Beasts, down-
load free screensavers and desktop wallpapers for
your computer, and even challenge your friends
to a Beast Tournament.

Sign up to the newsletter at www.beastquest.co.uk
to receive exclusive extra content and the oppor-
tunity to enter special members-only competitions.
We'll send you up-to-date info on all the Beast
Quest books, including the next exciting series
which features six brand-new Beasts!

Get 30% off all Beast Quest Books at www.beastquest.co.uk
Enter the code BEAST at the checkout.